BEST STORIES

FOR

UNDER FIVES

Also available from Hodder Story Collections

BEST STORIES

FOR

UNDER FIVES

BY CAROLYN HART
JULIA JARMAN
ANTONY LISHAK
TONY KENYON
SAM MCBRATNEY
VIVIAN FRENCH
FRANCESCA SIMON
AND JENNY KORALEK

Illustrated by Katy Rhodes

CONTENTS

James and Turner the Rabbit

Carolyn Hart

James and Turner the Rabbit

Carolyn Hart

"There was a rabbit in my class today," James told his mother while she was getting him ready for bed. "He was white with pink eyes and his name was Turner."

"I had a white rabbit once," said Mum. "His name was Sid, but I don't think he had pink eyes. Heavens James, either you've grown or these pyjamas have shrunk. I shall have to get you a new pair."

"Can I have some with Thunderbirds on?" asked James.

"Possibly," said his mother.

"Did Sid talk to you?" asked James as he ran round the room pretending to be an airplane.

"Not much," said his mother. "I don't think rabbits have a lot to say for themselves really."

"Turner does," said James, folding up his wings and climbing into bed.

During breakfast the next morning James told his mother that Turner came from Australia and had one hundred brothers and sisters.

"Who's Turner?" asked James' older sister, Bethan. "He sounds like a guy who needs help."

"Turner's a rabbit," said James with dignity. "A white rabbit with pink eyes. He sits next to me in class."

Bethan screamed with laughter. "You are silly," she told James. "Mum, he's so silly, he thinks rabbits go to school."

"Well, Turner does," said James,

sliding off his chair and heading for the door. "And he helps me with my sums."

That evening, after school, James told his mother that Turner wanted to come and live in their house.

"He says he's sick of living with one hundred other rabbits in Australia. He wants to live here."

"I don't know if there's room here for a rabbit," said James' mother. "Where would he sleep? What sort of things does he eat?"

"He can sleep in my room," said James. "And all he eats is courgettes."

"Well, I suppose it'll be OK," said James' mother doubtfully.

The next day Turner moved into Number 11 Wellington Crescent. He brought with him a yellow and black checked waistcoat, a pair of pink rubber boots and a large carrier bag of courgettes which James' mother stored in the bottom of the fridge.

"You can't sit there," James told

Bethan when she tried to climb onto the armchair to watch her favourite telly programme. "Turner's asleep there."

"Don't be ridiculous," said Bethan, sitting down anyway. But somehow the chair didn't feel as comfortable as usual, so she got up again.

"We can't eat that," James told his mother, when she put a large chicken casserole on the table. "Turner doesn't like it. He's a vegetarian."

"Well, give him a courgette and tell him to stop complaining," said James' mother crossly.

But somehow the casserole did not taste as good as it usually did.

"You can't have a bath," James told his father later. "Turner's in there trimming his whiskers."

"I don't care if the Duke of Edinburgh himself is in there," shouted his father. "I'm having a bath right now and that's all there is to it."

But somehow, having a bath while Turner trimmed his whiskers was not a relaxing experience.

By the end of the week everyone in James' family was fed up with Turner. Even James was beginning to think that a rabbit who only ate courgettes and spent all his time in the bathroom, or asleep in James' bed, was not much fun.

"That Turner's got to go," said James' father, rattling the newspaper crossly at breakfast. "I'm sick of living with a fat, opinionated rabbit who wears pink boots and cuts his whiskers in my bathroom."

"It would certainly be a relief not to have to think up any more courgette recipes," said James' mother. "Perhaps we could take him to the Zoo. He might prefer to stay in a place where there are lots of other animals."

So that afternoon, while Bethan visited her friend Sarah, and James' father cleaned out the garden shed, James and his mother took Turner to the Zoo. They introduced him to the Zoo rabbits, showed him the place where the Zoo rabbits slept and put his bag of courgettes carefully in a corner beside the Zoo rabbits' feeding bowls.

"It all looks very comfortable," said Mum hopefully. "I expect Turner'll be very happy here with his new friends."

"Yes," said James doubtfully. "But he says he's never slept on straw before . . ."

"Well, he'll soon get used to it," Mum said cheerfully as she bustled James away to find an ice-cream.

But when they got home, Turner was still there, sitting on Bethan's armchair reading a Disney annual.

"He thought the rabbits were stupid to stay in a Zoo when they could be outside living in a house," James reported. "Now he wants to watch Thunderbirds on the telly and eat a courgette."

"Maybe we should take him for a walk in the country," said Bethan. "He might find a lady rabbit and fall in love."

So on Sunday James' family took Turner for a long walk in the country. They showed him lots of rabbit holes and interesting plants for rabbits to nibble and stowed his waistcoat and wellingtons under a handy thornbush.

"It's certainly very peaceful," said James' father, looking round wistfully. "I wouldn't mind living here myself."

"Turner says he might have a little snooze in the sun," James told his family. "He'll catch us up later."

"No chance!" shouted Bethan. "Let's run back quick before he wakes up." They ran as fast as they could back down the track to the car and roared off home, but when they arrived, worn out and covered in mud – Turner was still there.

"He says 'where are the courgettes in the country?'" said James. "And he thinks it's too cold there when the sun goes in. He's gone to bed with a hot-water bottle and he doesn't want any supper."

"Well, I suppose that's something at least," groaned James' mother. "Does that mean we can have shepherd's pie tonight?"

After school on Monday James told his mother that Turner had said he was fed up with being ordered around at school and he wanted to go back to Australia to see all his brothers and sisters.

"Well, Calloo Callay," said James' mother. "What's he waiting for? Let's all go and say goodbye."

"But Mum, he can't get to Australia without a plane ticket," said James.

"Look here!" roared James' father when James' mother told him what Turner had said. "I'm not buying an invisible rabbit a plane ticket to Australia and that's that. The travel agent will think I'm stark raving bonkers. As far as I'm concerned he can walk to Australia."

11

"But rabbits can't walk that far," said James sadly. "Now he'll be here for ever."

"I know," said Bethan suddenly. "I've got an idea." She dashed out of the room. When she came back she handed James an envelope. "Here. Give this to Turner and see what he says." Inside the envelope was a piece of paper with: "One ticket to Australia. Single, no return. Departure today. Please bring luggage with you" written on it.

"He's very pleased," said James, when he had shown Turner his plane ticket. "He says 'thank you for having me, he's had a most enjoyable time' and now he's packed his things and he's waiting in the car for you to take him to the plane."

"Thank the Lord for that," said James' father as he drove them all to the airport to wave goodbye to Turner. "And now let's go and celebrate."

So they did.

Huffalo Buffalo

Julia Jarman

Huffalo Buffalo

Julia Jarman

Once upon a time in a land called Srilli-Puthur there lived a little buffalo, and this little buffalo was called Huffalo Buffalo, and he lived very near a coconut tree.

Now, one hot day, as little Huffalo Buffalo was sleeping beneath his coconut tree, something fell on his head.

"Help! Help! Help!" cried little Huffalo Buffalo.

"A piece of the sky just fell in my eye.
I must tell the Maharajah!" – and he
huff-hurried off to find him.

On his way Huffalo Buffalo met Babbity
Rabbit.
"Where are you going in such a hurry?"
asked Babbity Rabbit.
"Oh Babbity Rabbit!" cried Huffalo
Buffalo,
"Don't go that way!
A piece of sky just fell in my eye,
and I am off to tell the Maharajah!"
"Then I shall come too," said Babbity
Rabbit.
And Huffalo Buffalo and Babbity
Rabbit huff-hurried off to tell the
Maharajah.

On the way Huffalo Buffalo and Babbity
Rabbit met Hairy Scarey Bear.
"Where are you going in such a hurry?"
asked Hairy Scarey Bear.
"Oh, Hairy Scarey Bear!" cried Huffalo
Buffalo,
"Don't go that way!

A piece of the sky just fell in my eye,
and we are off to tell the Maharajah."

"Then I shall come too," said Hairy Scarey Bear.

So Huffalo Buffalo and Babbity Rabbit and Hairy Scarey Bear huff-hurried off to tell the Maharajah.

On the way Huffalo Buffalo and Babbity Rabbit and Hairy Scarey Bear met Hunkey Dunkey little red Monkey.

"Where are you all going in such a hurry?" asked Hunkey Dunkey little red Monkey!

"Oh, Hunkey Monkey!" cried Huffalo Buffalo,

"Don't go that way!

A piece of the sky just fell in my eye and we are off to tell the Maharajah."

"Then I shall come too," said Hunkey Dunkey little red Monkey.

So Huffalo Buffalo and Babbity Rabbit and Hairy Scarey Bear and Hunkey Dunkey little red Monkey all huff-hurried off to tell the Maharajah.

On the way Huffalo Buffalo and
Babbity Rabbit and Hairy Scarey Bear
and Hunkey Dunkey little red Monkey
met Snakey Lakey!

"Where are you all going in such a
hurry?" asked Snakey Lakey.

"Oh, Snakey Lakey!" cried Huffalo
Buffalo,

"Don't go that way! The sky is falling
down.

A piece of the sky just fell in my eye
and we are off to tell the Maharajah!"

"Then I shall come too," said Snakey
Lakey.

So Huffalo Buffalo and Babbity Rabbit and Hairy Scarey Bear and Hunkey Dunkey little red Monkey and Snakey Lakey all huff-hurried off to tell the Maharajah and on the way they met Pelly Welly Elephant.

"Oh Pelly Welly Elephant!" cried Huffalo Buffalo,

"Don't go that way! The sky is falling down.

A piece of the sky just fell in my eye and we are off to tell the Maharajah!"

"Then I shall come too," said Pelly Welly Elephant.

So Huffalo Buffalo and Babbity Rabbit and Hairy Scarey Bear and Hunkey Dunkey little red Monkey and Snakey Lakey and Pelly Welly Elephant all huff-hurried off to tell the Maharajah when suddenly they met Lion.

"STOP!" roared Lion.

"Now where are you all going in such a hurry?"

"Oh Lion!" cried Huffalo Buffalo,

"Don't go that way! The sky is falling down.

A piece of the sky just fell in my eye and we are off to tell the Maharajah!"

"Maha who?" roared Lion.

"Maha raja," said Huffalo Buffalo.

"Well," said Lion, "I know the Maharajah very well indeed. And I know that he would like to see this piece of the sky that fell in your eye. Have you got it with you?"

"N-no," said Huffalo Buffalo.

"Well, let's go back and get it," said Lion, and with that he started to run towards Huffalo Buffalo's tree.

"Oh Lion!" cried Huffalo Buffalo,

"Don't go that way! The sky is falling down.

A piece of sky just fell in my eye and we are off . . ."

"STOP!" roared Lion and he held up a paw.

"THAT'S ENOUGH-ALO,
HUFFALO BUFFALO!
Follow me!
Back to your tree."

Then Huffalo Buffalo and Babbity Rabbit and Hairy Scarey Bear and Hunkey Dunkey little red Monkey and Snakey Lakey and Pelly Welly Elephant all followed Lion back to the tree.

And Lion said, "I think the answer may be found

By looking carefully on the ground."

Then Huffalo Buffalo and Babbity Rabbit and Hairy Scarey Bear and Hunkey Dunkey little red Monkey and Snakey Lakey and Pelly Welly Elephant all looked on the ground and after a little while, Huffalo Buffalo said,

"Sorry folks, I've been a mut.

It wasn't a bit of sky, it was a coconut."

Then Babbity Rabbit and Hairy Scarey Bear and Hunkey Dunkey little red Monkey and Snakey Lakey and Pelly Welly Elephant and the Lion who was called Brian, all laughed and laughed – and so did Huffalo Buffalo.

The Battle of the Bedrooms

Antony Lishak

The Battle of the Bedrooms

Antony Lishak

Gemma and Gregory were twins. From the day they were born they did everything together. They ate together, shared the same toys, bathed together and slept in the same room. They even took turns in sleeping on the top bunk.

When they were five they held a party for all their friends. Everyone cheered and sang when they blew out the candles together. Everything was fine until it came to opening the presents.

Gregory got things that Gemma didn't like and Gemma got things that Gregory didn't like.

From that day on they started to play by themselves. Gregory played with his soldiers in one part of the room and Gemma played with her dolls in another. At first they were quite happy playing alone, but the peace didn't last for long.

"You're taking up too much room!" complained Gemma.

"But I need more space for my battles!" said Gregory.

"It's not fair!" said Gemma.

"I don't care!" said her brother.

"Oh please be quiet in there!" called their parents. But the trouble had only just begun.

Gemma and Gregory split their room into two parts. Gregory put all his things in one half and Gemma put hers in the other.

"You're not allowed over here!" said Gregory.

"I don't want to go there!" replied Gemma. "And you're not allowed over here!"

"Good!" said Gregory.

The argument carried on at bed time. They no longer wanted to share the top bunk. They both wanted to have it.

To stop all the squabbling their parents split the bunk bed into two and placed them as far apart as possible. It solved the problem of the beds, but there was worse to come.

They bickered over the bookshelves and divided them up. They quarrelled over the wardrobe and sectioned that up too. Soon the whole room was split. One half Gemma's, the other half Gregory's.

In the morning Gemma woke up to find a line of soldiers on the floor. "They are protecting my territory," explained Gregory. "So just keep out!"

"Right," thought Gemma. "This means war!"

That night Gregory found a spider in his bed! The next morning one of Gemma's dolls was on Gregory's side of the room, surrounded by soldiers. "I took her prisoner," said Gregory. "For trespassing!"

Then things went from bad to worse. First Gemma threw a ball of socks at her brother, then Gregory threw some pants back at her. Gemma hurled some vests at Gregory and he threw his pyjamas at her. Soon the room was a mess.

"What is going on in there?" called their parents.

"War!" shouted Gregory and more clothes missiles were thrown across the room.

"Stop it right now!" cried their parents.

"But I don't want to share a room with her any more!" said Gregory.

"Good!" snapped Gemma. "Because I don't want to share it with you either!"

To stop the fighting, their parents agreed to let them have their own rooms. So they cleared out the spare room and Gregory moved his bed, his toys and his clothes out of his old room and into the new one.

The twins had separated. The arguing had stopped. Both children had their own things in their own rooms. The Battle of the Bedroom was over.

But it was a cold, lonely night. Strange things happened. Gemma was woken by the sound of soft breathing. She looked down and there on the floor, huddled tightly in his bed covers, was her brother, snuggling next to her bed. Now there was peace.

Murdoch and the Toothache

Tony Kenyon

Murdoch and the Toothache

Tony Kenyon

One day Murdoch was cutting his toenails and eating chocolate when he felt an ache in one of his teeth.

"Ouch!" said Murdoch.

"You should brush your teeth more often," said his mother.

"But it takes too long," said Murdoch.

"Well it won't take long to make an appointment with the dentist," said his mother.

"It doesn't seem to be aching so much now," Murdoch said quickly.

"Your appointment is in thirty minutes," said his mother.

"I'm rather busy at the moment, I really must tidy up my room," said Murdoch.

"Here's your coat Murdoch, let's move it," said Mum, pushing a protesting Murdoch through the door.

"The dentist can see you now," said the receptionist when they arrived.

"Can he? I can't see him," said Murdoch.

"Come in young man," said a voice in the surgery.

"Don't be afraid," said Mum. "I'll give you a present if you are brave. It will all be over in a jiffy."

Murdoch opened the door and peered inside.

He glared at the dentist who dropped a tray of dentures on to the floor with a crash, and backed into a corner.

Instruments and files fell in all directions.

"But you're a crocodile," he cried!

"Yes," said Murdoch. "Been one all my life. Why are you shaking?"

"It's the teeth," said the dentist.

"You must be used to teeth by now," said Murdoch. "I've got a terrible ache in this long sharp one. I think you'd better take a look. Is this where I sit?" and he stretched out on the dentist's chair.

"I think I need to tidy my office," said the dentist.

"I've tried that excuse myself," said Murdoch.

"It doesn't work. This chair is very comfortable. Now come on! You must have done this a hundred times."

The dentist moved closer. "But there are so many teeth."

"Yes, crocodiles run out of energy brushing them you know."

"My, how your hands are shaking, have a gargle and calm down." Murdoch handed the dentist a glass of mouthwash.

"Now be brave, let's get the show on the road!"

After Murdoch had calmed the dentist down and wiped the sweat from his brow, the dentist took a deep breath. "Just a little cavity really, it won't take a second." And it didn't.

"I knew you could do it," said Murdoch. "You still look a bit pale though. I should lie down, I'll get you a cup of tea."

"A piece of cake for me," said Murdoch

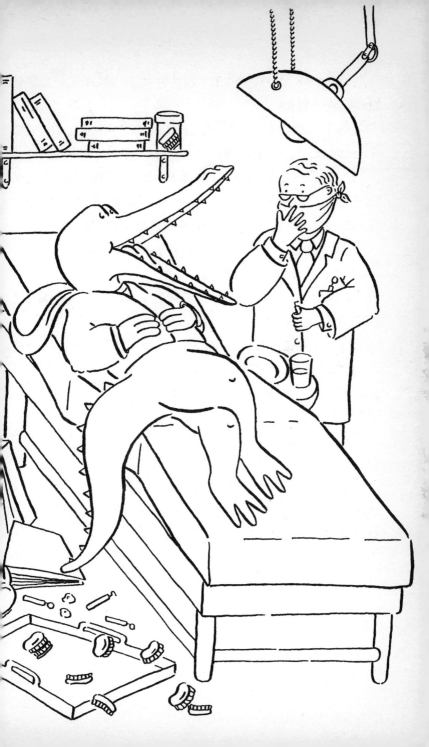

to the receptionist. "And a cup of tea for the dentist."

"You were brave Murdoch," said his mother. "I was worried when I heard the crashes, but you look very relaxed."

"Oh I'm very relaxed," said Murdoch. "But I'm not sure about the dentist. I think you had better give the present to him, he deserves it."

So they left a jar of pickled fish and seaweed with the receptionist.

"He should enjoy that with his cup of tea," said Murdoch.

Wasp Trouble

Sam McBratney

Wasp Trouble

Sam McBratney

Monty Ray was playing with his friends Shirley and Gordon when Myrtle Stackpole came along.

She was wearing a pink plaster on her knee. Monty wished that he had one too – he quite liked wearing plasters.

"Ha ha, I've got a plaster and you haven't," said Myrtle Stackpole.

"I don't care," said Monty.

"I bet you do," said Myrtle Stackpole.

41

Monty marched into his house. "Mummy, can I have a plaster, please?"

"What for?"

"Myrtle Stackpole has one on her knee."

"That's because she has a *cut* on her knee," said his mum. "She needs a plaster to keep the dirt out of it, so don't be silly and let's have some lunch."

After lunch, an awful thing happened. A wasp sneaked into Monty's house and stung his mummy. All of a sudden she said YEOW and grabbed her arm, and soon there was a big red mark where the wasp had jabbed her with its stinger.

"Is it sore?" asked Monty.

"Ooo. Well, it's quite sore," said his mother.

When Monty went out to play again he saw a wasp buzzing round his bin. That cheeky wasp! It had no business coming into his house and stinging his mummy like that. Boy, I'd like to zap that wasp, he was thinking as he picked up a big stick. This stick felt like a good

thing for zapping wasps.

"ZAP!" cried Monty, swinging wildly with the stick. "Zap, wap, zap!"

But the wasp didn't want to be zapped, and it wouldn't be still. It flew close to his ears with a loud bzzzz. Then it landed on his bare leg, and stung him.

When Monty ran into his house, he was howling as loudly as he could howl.

"Mummy, Mummy, I was zapping the wasp, I was zapping the wasp and it STUNG me on my sore leg."

"Such a thing to happen," said his mother as she put cream on the sting to take the pain away. She also told Monty that he shouldn't have been zapping the wasps.

"You'll only make them angry," she said.

"Do you think I should be a friend of the wasps?" asked Monty.

"Yes, you should. Well – not *too* friendly. Just leave them alone."

"And do you think I need a plaster to keep the dirt out of my sore leg?"

"That would be a good idea," said his mother.

Monty put a plaster on his sore leg. Then he put a plaster on his other leg. And he put a plaster on his cheek because it felt a bit itchy, and on his finger because there was a little cut there.

When Monty went out to play, he seemed to have plasters everywhere.

"What happened to you?" cried Shirley.

"I got stung by a wasp and I have to wear plasters," said Monty.

Myrtle Stackpole, who was only wearing *one* plaster, didn't say anything.

No Sleep for

Crocodile

Vivian French

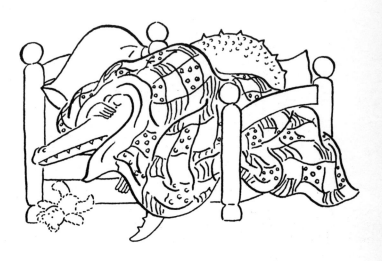

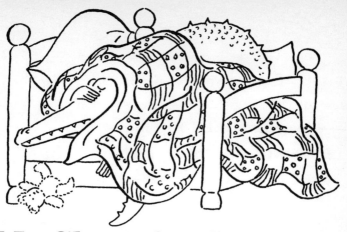

No Sleep for Crocodile

Vivian French

Crocodile couldn't get to sleep. Mother Crocodile had told him a story, and Father Crocodile had brought him a drink.

Mother Crocodile had sung him a song, and Father Crocodile had whistled him a tune.

It was no good. Crocodile tossed and turned and wriggled about, but he didn't feel sleepy at all.

"Just shut your eyes," said Mother Crocodile. "Shut your eyes and tell yourself a story. You'll soon be fast asleep."

Crocodile closed his eyes.

"I've shut my eyes," he said to himself. "Now I must tell myself a story."

Crocodile thought very hard for one whole minute. Then he opened his eyes again.

"I don't know any stories," he said.

Mother Crocodile sighed. "Yes you do," she said. "Think of the story I told you tonight."

"Oh yes," said Crocodile. He shut his eyes, and then opened them.

"I can't remember that one," he said. "Couldn't you tell it to me again? Then I'll go to sleep VERY quickly."

"No," said Mother Crocodile. "No more stories."

"What about a song?" asked Crocodile.

"No," said Mother Crocodile. "No more songs."

Crocodile was quiet for a moment. Then he looked at Father Crocodile.

"What about a tune?" he asked.

"No," said Father Crocodile. "No tunes either. If thinking of a story is too difficult just shut your eyes and think of something lovely. You'll soon be fast asleep."

"All right," said Crocodile. He shut his eyes.

"My eyes are shut," he said to himself. "Now I must think of something lovely."

Crocodile thought very hard for two whole minutes. Then he opened his eyes.

"Are monsters lovely?" he asked.

"I don't think so," said Father Crocodile.

"Oh," said Crocodile. "Because I can only think of monsters. Big fat hairy ones with long teeth and sharp claws."

Father Crocodile sighed. "If thinking of something lovely is too difficult," he said, "maybe you could shut your eyes and think of all the things you'd like for your birthday."

"All right," said Crocodile. He shut his eyes.

"My eyes are shut," he said to himself.

"Now I must think of all the things I want for my birthday."

Crocodile thought very hard for three whole minutes. Then he opened his eyes.

"When IS my birthday?" he asked.

There was no answer. Crocodile sat up. Mother Crocodile and Father Crocodile were both fast asleep.

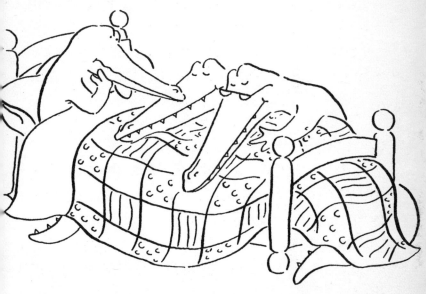

"Oh," said Crocodile. "I wonder if they thought of all the things they wanted for their birthday? Or if they told themselves a story? Or if they thought of something lovely?"

53

Crocodile lay down to think about it.

"I know what they thought about," he said, and he yawned. "They thought of something lovely."

He yawned again.

"They thought about ME," Crocodile said, and he closed his eyes and went to sleep.

Hugo and the Bullyfrogs

Francesca Simon

Hugo and the Bullyfrogs

Francesca Simon

Once upon a time there lived a very
small frog. His name was Hugo.

Hugo lived in a deep muddy pond.
Unfortunately for Hugo, other frogs lived
there too. Big frogs. Mean frogs. Grouchy
frogs. The biggest, meanest and
grouchiest frog of all was Pop Eyes.

Pop Eyes hopped around with a rough,
tough gang of bullfrogs.

The big bad bullfrogs swaggered

through the reeds, pushing and shoving and showing off. When the gang weren't pushing and shoving they liked to bellow together.

"Ribbet Ribbet flibbertigibbet," shrieked Pop Eyes.

"Croak Croak you're a joke," screeched Mudskipper.

"Brr-ack Brr-ack we're on the attack," rasped Puffy.

When the bullfrogs weren't making a hullabaloo, they liked to sneak up behind Hugo, lift him up, dangle him upside down and then drop him in the pond.

Hugo hated being pushed. He hated being shoved. Most of all he hated being dropped head first into the pond.

But what could Hugo do? He was so little.

He tried avoiding the gang.

He tried hiding.

He tried being friendly.

It was no use. The moment Hugo's back was turned, Pop Eyes would sneak up behind and shove him. Then he would lift Hugo up, drop him into the pond and the whole gang would laugh.

"Pipsqueak!"

"Squirt!"

"Tadpole!"

If Hugo was playing with a stick, Pop Eyes would snatch it.

If Hugo had a ball, Pop Eyes would kick it away.

If Hugo had a dandelion, Pop Eyes would blow it first.

Pop Eyes made Hugo's life horrid.

Everyone at the pond offered advice.

"The next time Pop Eyes drops you in the pond, splash him back," said the fish.

"I can't," said Hugo.

"The next time Pop Eyes shoves you, shove him back," said the dragonfly.

"I can't," said Hugo.

"The next time Pop Eyes pushes you, kick him," said the duck.

"I can't," said Hugo.

"Why not?" said the duck.

"My head tells my foot to kick, but my foot won't do it," said Hugo sadly.

"OK," said the duck. "Try this. When I push you, you shout, 'NO PUSHING!' "

The duck butted him with her bill.

"No pushing," whispered Hugo.

"Louder!" said the duck.

"No pushing," murmured Hugo, a little louder.

"I can't hear you," said the duck.

"No pushing," squeaked Hugo. "It's no use," he said. "I am a little frog, with a little croak."

The duck thought for a moment. "You do have a little croak," she said. "But

perhaps you have a loud quack."

"A loud quack?" said Hugo.

"Yes," said the duck. "Copy me."

And she quacked "NO PUSHING!" in her big loud strong duck voice.

Hugo puffed up his cheeks.

"Crr-Crr."

"Again!" said the duck.

Hugo pursed his lips.

"Qw-Qw."

"Again!" said the duck. "Open your mouth! You can do it!"

Hugo puffed up his cheeks as fat as he could. He pursed his lips as tight as he could. Then he opened his mouth as wide as he could and . . .

"QUACK!!! QUACK!!! QUACK!!!"

Birds scattered. Butterflies fluttered. Fish flapped.

Then Hugo heard a horrible hulla-baloo. Before he could hop off and hide, he was surrounded.

"Ribbet   Ribbet   flibbertigibbet," shrieked Pop Eyes.

"Croak Croak you're a joke," screeched Mudskipper.

"Brr-ack Brr-ack we're on the attack," rasped Puffy.

"Let's get him, boys!" shouted Pop Eyes.

Hugo puffed up his cheeks as fat as he could. He pursed his lips as tight as he could. Then he opened his mouth as wide as he could and . . .

"QUACK!!! QUACK!!! QUACK!!!" Which means, in duck, NO PUSHING!!!

For a moment there was silence.

Slowly the bullfrogs backed away.

"What did you say?" whispered Pop Eyes.

"I'm scared," murmured Mudskipper.

"I'm out of here," squeaked Puffy.

Hopping backwards, they slipped and fell head first into the pond.

"How did you do that?" asked Pop Eyes, as they all came spluttering to the surface.

"Do what?" said Hugo. "Oh, do you mean . . .

QUACK!!!"

And Pop Eyes, Mudskipper and Puffy fell in all over again.

Night Ride

Jenny Koralek

Night Ride

Jenny Koralek

I love it when we go to Nanna's in the night.

I love that night ride and the way it begins . . .

When we have supper on the early side . . .

And a lick and a promise instead of a bath . . .

And I put on my pink pyjamas
And my new lilac dressing gown

And my slippers with animals on . . .

And Mum puts little brother into my little old red dressing gown . . .

And Dad puts brother's bed into the back of the car in the boot . . .

Then scoops him up into his arms

And turns out the lights

And our house goes dark

And locks the front door

And our house goes quiet.

"Good-night, house," I say. "I'm coming back tomorrow."

Then I scuttle to the car in my animal slippers.

And climb by myself into my seat.

And Mum straps me in . . .

And gives brother his bottle . . .

I love the night ride to Nanna's house . . .

The car crawls along like a snail.

It's the rush hour

And everybody's going somewhere

And Mum and Dad sing silly songs

And brother drops his bottle on the floor and chatters on

Until he falls asleep.

And Mum says, "Ssh!" to Dad, "We'll wake the baby up."

And I sit back in the quiet and look and look at everything.

There's a crazy cat on the crossing

And oranges and lemons on the green fruit stall

And glowing red coals peeping out of holes where chestnuts are roasting . . .

Tired grown-ups look down on me from a big bus.

Sometimes they smile at me a bit and I smile back or wave.

Sometimes children make faces at me and I make faces back . . .

I love the night ride to Nanna's house . . .

I see black shapes against the sky . . . a black bird going to bed in a black tree . . .

And huge buildings like dark silent giants

And the tall clock tower which Mum says says "It's past seven o'clock and time you were in bed . . ."

And then comes the bridge, the bridge!
The best bit is the bridge with all its
thousand little lights it must have
borrowed from a thousand Christmas
trees which make the river gleam like
glass ...

I love the night ride to Nanna's house ...

When suddenly the rush hour's over
and suddenly I see the moon
And Dad goes faster for a while
Until we pass the park on the hill
Where I know tomorrow morning
Granpa will let me help him fly his kite.
We're nearly there and Dad slows down.
I know this corner!
I know this road!
I know this house!
There's Nanna at the window!
There's Granpa at the door.
Light pours out and I can see their
smiles.
I struggle up the path with brother's
folding mattress
"Hello, Nightrider," says Granpa. "Let

me give you a helping hand."

And we go up the steps and into the house to Nanna in the hall with two marshmallows on my own pink plate.

And Mum says, "Yes, all right, but you will have to clean your teeth again."

And Nanna comes with me to make sure I do

Then tucks me quickly into the bed that's always ready for me.

I love the night ride to Nanna's house . . .
I love the way it ends.

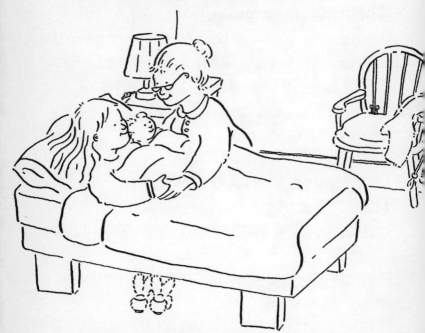

When Dad has put up brother's cot
And Mum has put him down in it,
When he's opened one eye and smiled
and shut it again,
When I've kissed Nanna and Granpa
And my Mum and my Dad,
When they've turned out the light
And whispered "Good-night,"
When I'm ready for sleep but not till
I've heard
Them laughing at one of Dad's jokes
And their voices talking softly
Through the open door.